GHOST DETECTORS

Spaced Out!

BOOK 18

BY
DOTTI ENDERLE

ILLUSTRATED BY
HOWARD MCWILLIAM

Calico

An Imprint of Magic Wagon
abdopublishing.com

For Rufus and Miles —HM

abdopublishing.com

Published by Magic Wagon, a division of ABDO, PO Box 398166,
Minneapolis, Minnesota 55439. Copyright © 2016 by Abdo
Consulting Group, Inc. International copyrights reserved in all
countries. No part of this book may be reproduced in any form
without written permission from the publisher. Calico™ is a
trademark and logo of Magic Wagon.

Printed in the United States of America, North Mankato, Minnesota.
032015
092015

 **THIS BOOK CONTAINS
RECYCLED MATERIALS**

Written by Dotti Enderle
Illustrated by Howard McWilliam
Edited by Rochelle Baltzer, Heidi M.D. Elston, Stephanie Finne &
        Bridget O'Brien
Designed by Jaime Martens & Jillian O'Brien

Library of Congress Cataloging-in-Publication Data

Enderle, Dotti, 1954- author.
  Spaced out! / by Dotti Enderle ; illustrated by Howard McWilliam.
      pages cm. -- (Ghost detectors ; book 18)
  Summary: Malcolm, Dandy, and Grandma Eunice go to SciCon to
meet the Ghost Stalkers--but when a ghost crashes the convention
the Stalkers' equipment is useless, and it is up to the boys to show
their heroes how it is really done.
  ISBN 978-1-62402-101-5
1. Ghost stories. 2. Science fiction--Congresses--Juvenile fiction.
3. Humorous stories. [1. Ghosts--Fiction. 2. Science fiction--Fiction.
3. Humorous stories.] I. McWilliam, Howard, 1977- illustrator. II.
Title. III. Series: Enderle, Dotti, 1954- Ghost Detectors ; bk. 18.
  PZ7.E69645Sp 2014
  813.6--dc23
                        2013027418

Contents

Chapter 1
SciCon

Of anything Malcolm ever wanted, this was what he wanted the most. The day had arrived. Soon he'd be at SciCon, a science fiction convention that draws thousands of fans each year. There would be celebrities. Lots of games. And lots of cool things to buy.

But this year was super special. The hosts of the reality TV show *Ghost Stalkers* would be there. Malcolm loved that show. Since he was also in the ghost-hunting

business, he couldn't wait to see them in person.

"We're ready to go," Malcolm said to his mom. He and his best friend and fellow ghost hunter, Dandy, stepped into the living room.

Malcolm's mom clapped her hands. "Oh my goodness, you guys look adorable!"

Adorable? That was not the reaction Malcolm had hoped for. Most everyone who attended SciCon dressed as a sci-fi or fantasy character. But Malcolm and Dandy decided to keep it real.

They dressed as the Ghost Detectors. The boys had become the Ghost Detectors after Malcolm bought an Ecto-Handheld-Automatic-Heat-Sensitive-Laser-Enhanced Specter Detector—a ghost finder that worked like a charm.

"We're not supposed to be adorable," Malcolm corrected his mom.

Malcolm had designed their uniforms. They wore brown cargo pants, red T-shirts, navy blue caps, and matching backpacks.

Using paint markers, Malcolm created a Ghost Detectors emblem on their T-shirts, caps, and backpacks. The emblem showed two stick figures with their arms crossed over their heads and a melting ghost with the word *Help!* in a speech bubble. Malcolm thought they looked great, not adorable.

"Quick," his mom said. "I want to take a picture of the cutest ten-year-olds at SciCon." She picked up her camera.

The boys struck the Ghost Detectors pose just like their emblem. Malcolm knitted his eyebrows and narrowed his eyes to show he meant business.

"Say cheese," his mom urged.

Malcolm slumped. "Mom, no one can say cheese and still look serious."

Click. She took the picture.

"Mom!" Malcolm complained. "I wasn't ready."

Click.

"Wait till I'm ready," he insisted.

Click.

He twisted his arms back over his head. "Ready, set—"

Click.

Malcolm struck the pose again and put on his most serious ghost-hunting face. But just as she took the picture, Dandy dropped his arm and scratched his nose.

Malcolm turned. "Dandy!"

"Sorry," Dandy apologized. "My nose was itchy."

WAVERLY PUBLIC LIBRARY

Click.

Malcolm sighed. "Never mind." He looked at his watch. "It's time to go."

"You have your tickets, right?" his mom asked.

The boys held them up, grinning.

Click. Malcolm didn't mind that picture.

"Come on," he said, motioning toward the door.

His mom tilted her head. "Hang on there. You're forgetting something."

Malcolm looked at Dandy. Dandy looked at Malcolm. They both shrugged. Malcolm asked, "Forgetting what?"

Right then, Malcolm's great-grandma came rolling through in her wheelchair.

"Woo-hoo!" Grandma Eunice shouted. She was wearing a white dress, a silver belt, and a gigantic pair of earmuffs. There

were huge reflectors on each side of her wheelchair. She pushed a button and—*whoosh*—it sounded like a fighter spacecraft.

Malcolm shook his head in disbelief. "Grandma Eunice is going with us?"

She patted her earmuffs. "I'm not Grandma Eunice. I'm Princess Leia."

Dandy nudged him. "How old is your great-grandma?"

"I'm not sure," Malcolm answered, "but I think she was born a long time ago in a galaxy far, far away."

"Okay, let's go," Malcolm's mom said.

Grandma Eunice pulled out a lightsaber that glowed neon green and buzzed a *wuhhh, wuhhh* noise when she moved it. "And may the Force be with us!"

Chapter 2
Heaven

Malcolm, Dandy, and Grandma Eunice waited outside the convention center. They were crammed within a mob of people dressed in wild costumes.

"How much longer?" Dandy asked. "I'm squished."

Malcolm wiggled his arm free so he could see his watch. "They should open the doors any minute."

Malcolm would be pacing if there was room to move around. He felt so anxious, his

heart was beating double-time. Although, that was probably because he could barely breathe. He was sandwiched in the crowd pretty tight.

Dandy was pinched between Wolverine and a fairy. When he turned one way, he got poked with metal claws. When he turned the other way, he got slapped in the face with a fairy wing.

"Once they open up the doors, I bet it will still take forever to get in," Dandy said to Malcolm.

Malcolm tried to shift away from the ogre standing next to him. Being a hairy beast was one thing, but did the guy have to smell like one, too?

"I don't know," Malcolm said, looking around. "I'm thinking this crowd will move pretty fast."

"I hope so," Grandma Eunice said, looking around. "I feel as trapped as a bird with salt on its tail."

Malcolm rolled his eyes. "Grandma, you can't trap a bird by putting salt on its tail. That's just an old saying."

Grandma Eunice raised an eyebrow. "Have you ever tried it?"

"No."

"Then you don't know if it works."

Malcolm sighed. "Never mind."

Right then, the doors opened. The mass of people stampeded inside to SciCon.

After a lot of yanking, tugging, and foot tromping, Malcolm, Dandy, and Grandma Eunice entered the convention hall. The crowd parted, forking off in different directions. Malcolm stood under the giant SciCon banner, gaping at all the booths.

"Which way should we go?" Dandy asked.

Grandma Eunice looked left and right. "Toward the restrooms." She patted her Princess Leia buns again. "I want to save the galaxy, but first I have to tinkle."

"Just hang on," Malcolm told her.

They wandered along, passing kooky space aliens and noble superheroes. A kid with a camera ran up to them and asked, "Who are you supposed to be?"

Malcolm and Dandy struck the pose. "We're the Ghost Detectors."

The boy blinked a few times. "Who are the Ghost Detectors?"

"Us," Malcolm said.

The boy squinted. "I mean, who are they really?"

"Us," Malcolm repeated.

The kid looked at Grandma Eunice. "Hey! Can I take your picture?"

"Sure," she answered. She flashed her dentures and the boy snapped the picture.

"Thanks!" he said.

She winked. "Print it out and I'll autograph it for you."

The boy nodded, then hurried away.

"Did that just happen?" Malcolm asked Dandy.

Dandy looked flabbergasted. "She's way too wrinkly to be Princess Leia."

Malcolm shrugged. "Maybe he thought she was Jabba the Hutt."

Grandma Eunice poked him with her lightsaber. "I heard that!"

He giggled.

They continued on, cruising from one table to the next. Malcolm was

overwhelmed. Everything he ever wanted was right here under one roof. A time travel compass. Miniature spybots. A Batman bottle opener. Bigfoot furry slippers. The list went on and on.

"Look," Malcolm said, picking up a *Ghost Stalkers* lunch bag. "Maybe one day our picture will be on a lunch bag, too."

"Yeah," Dandy agreed. "But until then, we can just draw ourselves on lunch sacks."

Malcolm gave him a look. "That's not the same."

After ten minutes of checking out the T-shirts, posters, and stickers—and finding the nearest ladies' room for Grandma Eunice—a voice boomed over the speakers, "The first of our celebrity panels will begin in five minutes. Join the Ghost Stalkers in Auditorium Three, where they'll discuss

their popular TV show, as well as answer your questions."

"Let's hurry," Malcolm said to Dandy. "I've got lots of questions. And who knows, we might even be able to give them some advice."

Chapter 3
An Ooky Love Story

"Come on, Grandma," Malcolm said. He looked around. "Grandma?"

Dandy pointed. "She's over there."

Two Jedi knights and a stormtrooper were standing next to her while a crowd of fans took pictures.

Malcolm couldn't believe it.

"I don't think she'll want to come with us," Dandy said.

Malcolm nodded. "I think you're right."

Auditorium Three was cold, stuffy, and dim, but Malcolm didn't mind. He and Dandy took seats in the middle of the large room.

On the stage was a long table draped with a white cloth. A pitcher of water and four clear glasses were set on it. Soon, Nick, Bob, and Carol of *Ghost Stalkers* walked in, lugging their ghost-hunting equipment.

They plopped the heavy gadgets onto the table, then each took their seats. Carol sat in the middle.

A man wearing faded jeans and a SciCon T-shirt sat beside them. "I'm Sheldon," he said into a microphone. "I'll be your moderator today."

There was some mild applause.

Malcolm was a little jealous. He would love to be in charge of a panel with the hosts of *Ghost Stalkers*.

Sheldon stroked the stubble on his chin. "I don't guess I need to introduce these guys."

The crowd rose, bursting into a frenzy of hoots and whistles. Malcolm and Dandy hooted and whistled the loudest.

"Then let's get down to business," Sheldon said.

He looked down at a stack of note cards in his hand. "Nick," he started.

Nick waved.

The crowd went crazy again. *Nick! Nick! Nick!*

Nick ran his fingers through his curly, dark hair and beamed.

When the noise died down, Sheldon continued, "Can you tell us how you got into the ghost-stalking business?"

Nick's eyes lit up like it was a heroic tale. "It was all by accident," he said with a shrug. "When I was in high school, I had a girlfriend named Wendy. She was sweet and beautiful and"—his cheeks blushed pink—"we were in love."

The crowd swooned. *Awww . . .*

Nick gazed off, dreamy-eyed. "We watched television together."

The crowd swooned again. *Oooh . . .*

"We went to movies together."

Awww . . .

"We studied together."

Oooh . . . Awww . . .

Malcolm nearly gagged. He wanted to hear about ghosts, not an ooky love story.

"But one night," Nick went on, "we were walking home from the big homecoming game." He smiled. "Our team won that night. I couldn't have been happier." Then his smile turned into a grimace.

"But I was no winner. I hadn't checked the weather forecast ahead of time. There were fierce wind gusts that night. Winds so strong we could barely walk. And to make matters worse, Wendy picked that night, of all nights, to wear a poncho."

The crowd gasped.

"We were just two blocks from her house," Nick said, "when a blast of air caught her and sent her sailing up like a runaway kite." He rubbed his forehead, distressed. "She was hovering above the trees. The drop was so far."

Nick closed his eyes and pinched the bridge of his nose like the memory was too painful. "Who knew that on that windy night, my Wendy would wind up . . ." His voice choked and he sniffed back tears.

The crowd swooned again. *Oooh . . . Awww . . .*

Malcolm tried to imagine Wendy soaring like a glider with poncho wings.

"I thought I'd lost her that night," Nick said. "But then, two weeks later, I started dating a girl named Darcy. Wendy's ghost showed up and, wow, was she furious!

She jabbed me in the eyes, then ripped out a chunk of Darcy's hair. I couldn't believe it! How could someone so sweet when she was alive be so vicious after death? All that violence was so uncalled for."

The crowd mumbled in agreement.

"Seriously, why was she so upset?" Nick continued. "I didn't tell her to wear a poncho that night. And why didn't she check the weather report? I mean, really, that wind was so strong it could uproot trees. You would think she would have thought of that."

"So what happened?" Sheldon urged.

"Wendy haunted me for two whole days. So," Nick held up a large gizmo that looked like a leaf blower, "I bought an Ace-Fifteen-High-Powered-Electromagnetic Ghost Blaster. I shot her straight back to

the spirit world." He pumped his fist. "I've been a Ghost Stalker ever since."

The crowd went wild.

"That thing is cool," Dandy said.

"Yeah," Malcolm agreed, "but not very portable. It definitely wouldn't fit in a backpack."

Sheldon flipped to another note card. "Carol, how did you get into the ghost biz?" he asked.

She shrugged. "Bought some equipment and hung out in haunted houses."

"Cool," Sheldon said. Then he looked at Bob. "How about you, Bob?"

Bob nodded toward Carol. "I did what she did."

The crowd applauded like they were truly amazed.

"Awesome," Sheldon said, thumbing through his cards.

The Ghost Stalkers sipped water, showed off their ghost gadgets, and discussed specific episodes.

Thirty minutes later, Sheldon ran out of note cards. He turned to the crowd. "It's time to take questions from the audience."

Malcolm's hand immediately shot up.

Chapter 4
Just $7.95 Each

"**R**ats!" Malcolm said, looking around the room. A gazillion other hands were raised, too. "I'll never get their attention."

"Wiggle your fingers," Dandy suggested. "That usually works for me."

Malcolm wiggled his fingers.

Sheldon glanced out at the crowd, his head sweeping right to left. Then he pointed to a girl in the first row dressed as Wonder Woman.

"Hey," Sheldon said with a smile, "what's your name?"

She adjusted her plastic tiara. "I'm Diana."

Malcolm whispered to Dandy, "In the comic books, Wonder Woman's real name is Diana. I bet that lady made it up."

"My question is for Nick," Diana said.

Nick took a sip of water, playing it cool.

With a flirty voice, she asked, "Do you have a girlfriend now?"

A wave of *oohs* rose from the crowd.

Malcolm rolled his eyes. "Who cares about that?"

Dandy shrugged. "I guess Wonder Woman does."

Malcolm crossed his arms and huffed. "Why are they wasting time on dumb questions?"

Nick didn't seem to mind it. He grinned, pretending to be shy. "At the moment," he batted his thick, dark eyelashes, "there is no special love in my life."

This triggered some major swooning among the ladies in the audience.

Malcolm blew out some nervous air. "Unless you count his reflection in the mirror."

Carol's brows dipped. She turned to Nick. "What about Philomena in our editing department? I thought you were seeing her."

Bob sat back, looking puzzled. "Philomena? I thought he was seeing Tiffany in the mail room."

Nick's tanned cheeks burned bright red. His eyes ticked back and forth as he squirmed, trying to come up with

something to say. "Uh . . . let's move on to the next question, okay?"

Sheldon scanned the crowd. Malcolm stood on his tiptoes and wiggled his fingers.

Sheldon pointed to a guy wearing cellophane bags full of raspberry Jell-O. "What are you supposed to be?" he asked the guy.

The man stepped into the aisle and wiggled. "Can't you tell?"

Sheldon shook his head. "You look like the cranberry sauce my granny slaps on my plate every Thanksgiving."

The crowd boomed with laughter.

The guy laid down on the floor and rolled. People ducked in case one of the bags exploded. No one wanted to get slimed with Jell-O.

Sheldon shrugged. "I give up."

The guy heaved himself off the floor. "I'm the Blob!"

"Oh . . . ," Sheldon said, eyes wide, like it suddenly made sense.

"He looks more like Granny's cranberry sauce to me," Dandy whispered to Malcolm, giggling.

"Yeah," Malcolm agreed.

"So what's your name and what's your question?" Sheldon asked.

"My name is Steve McQueen," the guy answered.

Malcolm rolled his eyes again, then whispered to Dandy, "Steve McQueen is the actor who starred in the movie *The Blob*. Why can't these people just use their real names?"

"Here's my question," the Blob continued. "How do I get rid of a stink ghost?"

Carol leaned forward, her eyebrows dipped. "Excuse me?"

"I'm being haunted by a stink ghost," he repeated. "My house smells like an unflushed toilet."

"Do you know for sure it's a ghost?" Bob asked.

"Yeah," the Blob assured him. He jiggled as he counted off each clue with his fingers. "It hides my air freshener. It blows out my aroma candles. And it dumps garlic in my potpourri. It's so gross. I have to walk around with a clothespin on my nose."

The crowd turned back to the Ghost Stalkers, eager to hear the answer.

"Here's what you do," Bob said. "First, you buy some of these." He showed off a few metal disks that blinked blue and yellow lights. "They're called Spook Sensors. They pick up any spirit activity in the room."

The Blob pulled out a pen and note pad to jot it down.

"Next," Bob went on, "you want to buy one of these." He held up something that looked like a spray gun. "This is a Phantom

Freezer. When the Spook Sensors start to blink, just quickly spray this. It'll stop the ghost in its tracks."

"Stop. Ghost. In. Tracks," the Blob repeated as he wrote it down.

Then Bob held up something that looked like a very large electrified fork. "This is called a Ghost Roaster." He turned it front and back, then pulled a trigger. White sparks spewed out of the end of it. "Once your phantom is frozen, jab it with the roaster. It'll crumble into pieces and disappear."

"Wow, that's great!" the Blob said. "Where can I buy those things?"

"All of these gadgets and more are available on the *Ghost Stalkers* website."

The Blob jiggled with joy. "How much do they cost?"

"Just $7.95 each," Nick answered with a smile. "Plus shipping and handling."

"But!" Carol quickly added, "If you buy all three, you get a ten-dollar discount and a free *Ghost Stalkers* T-shirt."

The Blob drooped. "Oh . . . uh . . . thanks."

Dandy nudged Malcolm. "It's cheaper to buy clothespins."

Sheldon clapped his hands, eager to move on. "Any more questions?"

Malcolm was desperate. He stood on his chair and wildly wiggled his fingers. It

worked. Sheldon glanced around the room, then pointed to him. "How about you?"

Malcolm checked behind him to make sure Sheldon was talking to him.

"You," Sheldon said again, "in the red shirt. Do you have a question?"

Malcolm grinned. "I have several."

Chapter 5
Just Adorable

Malcolm remained standing on the chair. "My name is Malcolm."

People looked at each other like they were trying to remember a superhero or sci-fi character named Malcolm.

"That's my real name," he added.

"Then who are you dressed like?" Bob asked.

Malcolm motioned to Dandy. Dandy stood up on his chair, too. They beamed. "We're the Ghost Detectors."

Carol clapped. "How adorable!"

Malcolm cringed. "No, we're not adorable."

"I think you are," she said, a big grin spreading across her face.

There was no point in arguing. "First," Malcolm told her, "I'm a huge fan of the show."

"Thank you," Carol said. Bob and Nick smiled.

Nick looked at his watch. "So what's your question?"

Malcolm fidgeted a little. "It's not really a question. It's just that . . . you seem to do things the hard way. There are easier ways to track and remove a ghost."

The crowd burst into laughter.

"How would you know?" Bob asked, smirking.

"Because," Malcolm answered, "we're ghost hunters, too."

"That's just so adorable," Carol repeated.

Malcolm shook his head. "There's nothing adorable about dealing with ghosts. Some are lonely. Some are lost. Some are vicious. And some are just annoying."

"You can say that again!" the Blob shouted.

"We know all of this," Nick said. "We've gotten rid of hundreds of ghosts."

The show had been on the air for two seasons. The way Malcolm remembered it, they'd gotten rid of maybe fifteen ghosts. The rest of the ghosts made fast getaways, and some investigations turned up nothing. Maybe Nick was counting ghosts they hunted before they became famous.

"My friend Dandy and I have gotten rid of a bunch, too," Malcolm said.

Dandy waved. "Yeah. We've been around a lot of scary stuff."

Several people in the crowd yawned.

"Seriously," Malcolm said, "you don't need all that expensive equipment."

Nick drummed his fingertips on the table. "You do if you want to do the job right."

Malcolm turned to the Blob. "If you want to get rid of your stink ghost, just put some potpourri in a coffee can. Then pour in some honey. When the ghost puts the garlic inside, it'll get stuck. All you need to do is pop on the lid and bury it in the yard. It's simple."

The Blob nodded. "Hey, that could work."

Bob was starting to sweat. "But maybe not. Remember, our ghost equipment is guaranteed."

"Guaranteed to clean out my bank account," the Blob snapped.

Bob glared at Malcolm. "Did you come here to insult us, kid?"

"No! Like I said, I'm a huge fan," Malcolm repeated.

"Then ask a real question or sit down."

There were nods from the crowd.

Malcolm took a deep breath. "I'd like to know why you don't use more valuable equipment, like the Ecto-Handheld-Automatic-Heat-Sensitive-Laser-Enhanced Specter Detector," he said. "We've drawn out a lot of ghosts with that thing."

"And we use a ghost zapper that can wipe out the pesky ghosts," Dandy added.

"We don't play with toys," Bob huffed, crossing his arms.

"They're not toys," Malcolm said. "I can show you."

Before Malcolm could unzip his backpack, Carol squinted at him. "Wait, I know who you are."

Malcolm froze. "You do?"

She pointed a menacing finger. "You're that kid who writes to us every week telling us how to do our job."

The crowd turned, giving Malcolm the stink eye. *Boooo! Hissss!*

"I'm not trying to tell you how to do your job," Malcolm defended. "I'm just trying to make it easier for you."

Malcolm looked at Nick. "Think about it. That detecting rod you use is really long and heavy. How many times has a ghost

taken it away and bopped you over the head with it?"

"Hey, that only happened once," said Nick.

"Because you ducked the other times," Dandy added.

Sheldon rapped the table with his hand, then stood. "Enough. I think it's time to move on. There are a lot of people with real questions."

"But," Malcolm said, "I'm just trying—"

"Stop talking," Sheldon insisted, "or we'll have you removed from this room."

Malcolm sighed.

"Look, kid," Bob said, "I get it. Playing Ghost Stalkers is fun." He winked at Malcolm. "But it's safer to play this." He held up a small video game box. *"Ghost Stalkers: The Home Game."*

Malcolm slumped and dropped back down in his chair. There was no point in responding.

Dandy hopped down too. "You've got to admit, they are the professionals."

Malcolm shook his head. "I don't know. I'm starting to think they're just actors putting on a fancy show."

Chapter 6
The SciCon Ghost

After the panel discussion, the Ghost Stalkers hurried out a side door. Sheldon rose. "Bob, Carol, and Nick will be in the convention hall in ten minutes to sign copies of their newest book, *When the Haunts Go Marching In*. Make sure you pick up a copy."

"Are we going to buy one?" Dandy asked Malcolm.

Malcolm shrugged. "Might as well. They are the main reason we came here."

"Just don't give them any more advice about ghost hunting," Dandy warned.

Malcolm adjusted his backpack on his shoulders. "They wouldn't listen anyway."

The boys poured out with the crowd. Malcolm looked around. "We need to find Grandma Eunice."

Dandy pointed. "She's right over there."

People were watching her pop wheelies in her wheelchair. A girl with green skin and braids shouted, "Go Leia! Go Leia!"

A guy dressed like a troll shouted, "That's one hot granny!"

Malcolm closed his eyes and shook his head. "This is so embarrassing." He and Dandy trudged over.

"There you are," Grandma Eunice said, winking. "Did you see me defeat Darth Vader?" She nodded toward a booth.

A crinkled cutout of Darth Vader lay on the ground, tire marks streaking it. A guy dressed like Luke Skywalker stood next to it, shaking his fist at them. "She owes me twenty bucks for this!"

"Relax," Grandma Eunice said. "It's not like I plowed down your father." Then she turned to Malcolm. "I wish you boys hadn't missed that. The Force was with me."

"We were at the *Ghost Stalkers* panel," Malcolm told her.

Grandma Eunice's face lit up and she clacked her dentures. "I love the Ghost Stalkers! That Nick is one cutie-patootie."

Malcolm rolled his eyes. "Dandy and I are going to get an autographed copy of their book. Where will you be?"

"I'll be in the restroom. Overthrowing a dark lord like Vader makes me have to

tinkle. But first," she said, pointing toward Luke Skywalker, "I have to pay this guy twenty bucks." A smile crept across her face. "It was worth every penny."

"Try to stay out of trouble," Malcolm warned.

The boys rushed across the convention floor and took their places in the Ghost Stalkers' line. The Blob jiggled up to them. "Hey, Malcolm, I'm going to try your method. Clothespins on the nose are awfully painful."

"It should work," Malcolm said. "But if it doesn't, call us." He handed over one of his Ghost Detectors business cards.

"Yeah," Dandy agreed. "We'll get rid of that stinker fast."

Even though Sheldon kept the line moving, it was still slow going. It took

forever, but Malcolm and Dandy finally made it to the Ghost Stalkers' table.

Carol signed the book for Malcolm and passed it to Bob.

Bob curled his lip at Malcolm while he signed. Then he slid the book over to Nick. "Hey, Nick," he said, "take a look. I managed to write my name without this kid telling me how to do it."

Carol sighed. "Oh hush, Bob. I think these boys are adorable."

Malcolm rolled his eyes.

Nick scribbled his name in the book. "Thanks, kids. Good luck with your ghost hunting." He slid the book toward Malcolm. But just as Malcolm reached for it, the book slid back.

Nick slid it to Malcolm again. "Take it."

Malcolm tried. The book slid back.

"Do you want it or not?" Nick griped. "People are waiting."

Malcolm snatched at it, but the book slid to the right. When Dandy made a grab for it, the book slid to the left. Now all three of the Ghost Stalkers were watching.

"Is this some kind of trick?" Nick asked, glaring at Malcolm.

Malcolm shook his head. "No. Something's moving it."

The book flew up and bopped Nick in the nose. "Ow!" He quickly reached in his pocket and pulled out a small mirror. "Not my face!"

The book whacked him again.

"Ouch!" He checked the mirror again. "Is my nose bleeding?"

Bob slammed his fists on the table and stood. "Stop it, kid, or we'll call security."

"I'm not doing it!" Malcolm insisted.

Whoosh! A strong wind swept across the table. The books toppled over like dominoes.

The line of people jumped back, eyes wide.

"What's going on here?" Sheldon asked, glaring at Malcolm.

Malcolm threw his hands in the air. "It's not me!"

"He's right," Bob said. He gleamed at the crowd. "Looks like we've got ourselves a genuine SciCon ghost."

He'd barely finished his announcement when the marker he'd been using rose in the air and drew a big, black mustache on his upper lip. He swatted at it, but it was too late. Bob looked like a villain from an old black-and-white movie.

"That's a good look for him," Dandy whispered to Malcolm.

Malcolm would've agreed, but he was too busy keeping an eye on the situation.

Everyone should've been scattering, panicked. But instead they lifted their cameras and snapped picture after picture.

Carol managed to snatch the marker. Holding it tight, she said, "Ha-ha. This

ghost seems to have a real sense of humor."
That's when the sprightly spook grabbed a
handful of her hair. It twisted and twisted,
winding her hair on top of her head and
raising her up off of her chair.

"Hey!" she griped.

Suddenly, it stopped. Carol's eyes
bulged as her hair unwound, spinning her
round and round like a dangling yo-yo.
When she dropped back down, her head
lolled in circles and her cheeks puffed like
she might throw up.

Nick ducked, but not quick enough. The
ghost grabbed his collar and tugged him
forward. "Please," Nick begged, "not my
hair!"

But that didn't stop the ghost. Out
of nowhere, a nasty glop of ectoplasm
plopped on top of Nick's head. The green

gunk oozed down like gravy on mashed potatoes.

"So much for being a cutie-patootie," Dandy said.

Bob looked at his two partners, then narrowed his eyes. "No ghost is going to outsmart us!" Then, with his hands on his hips, he said, "Stand back, folks. It's time for the Ghost Stalkers to get to work."

Chapter 7
Say Good-bye

The crowd backed up a little, but they continued taking pictures and recording the action.

Carol stood, her hair hanging in a giant knot. "Sheldon, please get our equipment . . . NOW!"

Dandy turned to Malcolm. "Cool! I bet they'll film this for their show."

"Of course," Malcolm said, shaking his head in disgust. "They're not going to pass this up."

Suddenly, the convention hall rumbled and quaked, trembling like a freight train was passing through.

Malcolm braced himself. "Uh-oh. This can't be good."

"Where are the cameras?" Bob shouted. "This should be documented!"

That's when everything exploded. People fell to the floor, and every SciCon display was sent shooting into the air.

"You're right," Dandy said, trying to pick himself up. "Nothing good about that."

People panicked, tromping over each other, racing for the exits. Sheldon and a film crew bulldozed through, pushing a large cart full of *Ghost Stalkers* gizmos.

"Everyone, clear out!" Carol yelled. "It's too dangerous."

But quite a few people stayed back.

Dandy's face turned sour. "Malcolm, maybe we should get out of here."

Grandma Eunice wheeled up, waving her lightsaber. "I haven't had this much fun since I won three jackpots at bingo last month."

"Grandma," Malcolm said, "you should go. You could get hurt."

"No way!" Grandma Eunice argued. "I want to see how the Ghost Stalkers handle this case." She smiled and winked at Nick. "Go get 'em, cutie-patootie!"

Malcolm grabbed her wheelchair and pulled her back. "Shhh! Let's stay quiet so they don't make us leave."

Grandma Eunice made a motion like she was zipping her lips.

The three of them moved back, finding a quiet corner.

"I . . . I . . . don't think this is a good idea," Dandy stammered. "Maybe we should just wait and watch it on TV."

Malcolm placed his hand over Dandy's mouth. "Shhh."

Nick looked at the cameraman. "Are we rolling?"

The cameraman gave a thumbs-up.

Nick straightened his shirt. Then he gazed seriously into the camera. "As you can see, what should have been a great day turned out to be a near-deadly disaster here at SciCon."

Malcolm looked around. He wouldn't describe it as near deadly.

"Luckily," Nick said, "the Ghost Stalkers are on the case."

Bob stepped in front of the camera. He'd tried to wipe away his marker mustache,

but a shadow of it remained. "Come on, Nick, let's nab this thing."

Carol joined them, and they each held a *Ghost Stalkers* gadget as they crept along.

"Yoo-hoo. I know you're in here," Bob called to the ghost.

The room was amazingly quiet.

They stopped. Bob looked at Nick. "Is it still here?"

Nick checked the color on his ghost radar. "It's still here."

Everyone glanced around. Even the cameraman checked over his shoulder.

Carol, Bob, and Nick stayed close, scanning the room. They had barely taken three steps when a popcorn machine exploded. *Ping, ping, ping, ping!* Pellets of undercooked kernels hit them.

"Ouch!" Bob cried.

Dandy scrunched his face and looked at Malcolm. "Maybe they should wear armor."

"Or use some of that high-dollar equipment," Malcolm added.

Just then, comic books flapped and flew like birds. Remote control UFOs whirled to life. Several robots lit up and marched forward.

"Wow," Malcolm said. "This thing's all over the place."

Bob stepped forward. "We've got to see what we're dealing with here." He raised a long, silver pole with circling lights, then smiled into the camera. "This ghost radar will show us what type of demon we're dealing with."

Bob edged across the messy room, the pole towering over his head. The colorful lights rotated round and round, then finally stopped on purple.

"Just what I thought." Bob turned to the camera. "We're dealing with a Level Five Blue-tailed Bogeyman."

Grandma Eunice clapped her hands excitedly. "Woo-hoo!" she yelled. "And it's a nasty one, too."

"Shhh!" Malcolm warned.

Grandma Eunice laughed. "I'm not scared of that thing."

Nick rushed over to Bob. "I'll put a tracker on it." He held up something that looked like a giant slingshot. When the ghost swept across a stack of X-Men T-shirts, Nick aimed. A teeny pulsating dot shot up and stuck to the ghost.

"You can't hide now!" Nick yelled to the bogeyman.

"This calls for a Spirit Spoiler," said Carol. She held up something that looked like a bicycle wheel. She flipped a switch and the wheel began spinning at blurring speed. She flipped another switch and the gadget made a suction sound.

"I've seen them use this before," Malcolm whispered to Dandy. "It works like the ghost scooper I made out of a dust

buster. Only they probably paid a thousand dollars for theirs."

It was easy to spot the ghost. The tiny little sensor light flitted like a bee all over the room. It settled in front of Grandma Eunice. She held up her lightsaber and flipped a switch. The ghost must have liked the green glow. It grew closer . . . and closer . . . and closer . . . then—*whack!* She swatted it hard. The light shot away like she'd hit a home run.

"The Force is with me, you bungling bogeyman!" Grandma Eunice shouted.

But that only stopped it for a moment. The ghost flew near the entrance, where some SciCon fans were hanging out.

A guy dressed as Spider-Man stepped up. "I'll get it." He held out his wrist and shot a sticky wad of webbing at it. But the

fake web was nothing but Silly String. The ghost managed to grab it and tug. It flung Spidey onto a broken table full of pies and cupcakes.

"Let the professionals do this!" Bob shouted. The three Ghost Stalkers charged at the ghost, the Spirit Spoiler whirling.

But the ghost was too quick. It ping-ponged off the walls, the floor, and the ceiling.

"It's a little speed demon," Dandy said.

Then suddenly the ghost stopped. It hovered directly in front of the Ghost Stalkers.

"Say good-bye, Bogeyman," Nick said, grinning.

It can't be this easy, Malcolm thought.

Chapter 8
To the Rescue

Nick motioned for the cameraman to move in closer. The ghost remained, light flashing. Then everything happened at once.

As the cameraman inched up, the bogeyman looped in the air, grabbed the camera cord, and wound it round and round the cameraman. "Help!" the guy shouted as the ghost tied him to a pole.

Carol ran, swinging the Spirit Spoiler, trying to suck in the spook. But it grabbed

the gadget and flipped the reverse switch. The spoiler whirled like a propeller, sending Carol helicoptering up. She landed on a window up near the ceiling.

"Hey!" Carol shouted. "Somebody get me down from here!"

Then the ghost snatched up the slingshot and a pile of sensors. Like rapid fire, it shot one after another at Bob. He hopped and danced—"Ow! Ow!"—as the twinkling sensors stuck to him.

"Whee doggies!" Grandma Eunice hooted. "He's flashier than a Christmas tree!"

When Bob tried picking the sticky little lights off, the ghost floated over and dropped a giant gob of gooey ectoplasm on top of him, gluing him to the floor.

"That's never going to wash off," Dandy said.

Nick's face turned as white as a peeled potato when the bogeyman headed toward him. "No!" he yelled, backing away.

The ghost showed no mercy. It dropped a SciCon souvenir rain poncho over Nick. Then, it blew a strong breath that sent him sailing into the air, just like his old girlfriend, Wendy.

"Ahhhh!" Nick ended up dangling from the jumbotron, where he clung for dear life.

The bogeyman then picked up Thor's hammer and began pounding everything that wasn't already destroyed.

Dandy turned to Malcolm. "I don't think this episode is going to have a happy ending."

Malcolm shrugged his backpack off his shoulders. "Yeah, it will." He took out his trusty ghost detector and powered it on.

Bleep-bleep-bleep. The bogeyman instantly appeared.

Grandma Eunice clacked her dentures. "Whoo-whee, that's an ugly one!"

Was it ever! Malcolm thought.

Hovering before them was a nasty blue blob as wrinkly as a hound dog. It had a huge nose, gigantic ears, stubby little arms, and a curlicue tail. The sensor was stuck

to its forehead, winking like a third eye. Malcolm had never seen anything like it.

Dandy's lip curled. "Ew, gross. That's a Blue-tailed Bogeyman?"

"Yeah," Malcolm said. "But not for long." He took out the ghost zapper and tossed it to Dandy. "Zap that hideous lump."

Dandy aimed and—*splat!*—sprayed zapper juice all over an Iron Man poster about ten feet away. The bogeyman had zoomed to the left.

Dandy aimed again. But the bogeyman zoomed to the right. Then it went up. Then down. Then up again. It zigzagged too fast for him!

"It's too fast!" Dandy complained.

"Kid!" Nick yelled from the jumbotron. "If you can destroy that thing, do it! I don't know how much longer I can hang on."

After all the advice Malcolm had given the Ghost Stalkers, he couldn't mess this up now. He had to prove he knew what he was doing.

"So what now?" Dandy asked.

Good question, Malcolm thought. But then he raised an eyebrow. "I've got an idea." He handed the ghost detector to Dandy. "Keep an eye on it."

Malcolm waded through the SciCon disaster. He kicked aside books, action figures, and battle-axes in search of the one thing he needed. He found it next to the popcorn machine. He hid it inside his backpack and ran back to the scene.

The convention center was still and quiet. The Ghost Stalkers watched and waited. They were counting on him. He couldn't fail now.

The bogeyman zoomed round and round in figure eights with a huge grin on its face.

"I don't like this," Dandy whispered. "He's planning something."

"So am I," Malcolm said.

Malcolm inched closer to Grandma Eunice. "Where's your lightsaber?"

She held it up. "You want me to whack that bogeyman again?"

Malcolm shook his head. "No, just turn it on."

She did. It glowed to life with a *wuhhh, wuhhh*. The bogeyman grew close to it.

"It's mesmerized by it," Dandy said.

Malcolm carefully reached into his backpack. "I know."

He crept around the ghost, slipped up behind it, then pulled out a large tin saltshaker. Right then, the bogeyman knew

something was up. But before it could make a quick getaway, Malcolm opened the shaker and dumped a big pile of salt on the bogeyman's blue tail.

The ghost tried to shoot away, but the salt weighed it down. The bogeyman could only spin in circles.

"Quick!" Malcolm yelled to Dandy.

Dandy tossed him the zapper. Malcolm didn't waste a second spraying the purple goo on the ghost. The bogeyman froze, its beady eyes wide. Then it melted like ice cream in the sun. The only thing left was the blinking sensor that plinked to the floor.

"That was some superduper goblin catching," Grandma Eunice said.

The folks left in the room cheered. Except the Ghost Stalkers.

Malcolm and Dandy rushed over to where Bob and the cameraman were trapped.

"To the rescue," Malcolm said to them with a smile. "Although . . ." He looked up at Carol and Nick. "I don't know how we're going to get them down."

"Do something!" Nick cried. "My fingers are slipping!"

Chapter 9
Got the Message

Malcolm, Dandy, and Grandma Eunice sat in front of the TV. All week, they had seen commercials for the new *Ghost Stalkers* episode, "Demon Disaster at SciCon."

"I can't wait!" Grandma Eunice said.

"Yeah," Dandy agreed. "We're going to be superstars!"

The episode started with Bob, Carol, and Nick sitting on a comfy couch in a studio. They all wore grim faces.

"As you'll see," Bob began, "this was our worst haunting yet. They may never hold another SciCon again."

The scene faded to inside the convention center. Malcolm sat forward, eyes glued to the TV. "Here we go."

It showed the convention center rumbling and quaking.

"Wait," Dandy said, pointing. "They cut out the part where the ghost draws a mustache on Bob."

Next, it showed the Ghost Stalkers creeping along, Bob holding up the radar. It cut to Nick putting the tracker on the ghost, then Carol with the Spirit Spoiler.

Bob's voice sounded over the film. "Some amateurs tried to stop it."

It showed Grandma Eunice batting off the ghost.

"Grandma, it's you!" Malcolm shouted.

"Wow! I look exactly like Princess Leia." Dandy giggled.

Next, it showed Spider-Man trying to web the spirit.

Bob's voice came on again. "The beast finally decided to show itself."

"Decided?" Malcolm said.

The next scene was Dandy trying to zap the ghost.

"Hey!" Dandy griped. "That's not how it happened."

The camera cut to the convention catastrophe. "See what a Blue-tailed Bogeyman can do?" Bob said. "Thank goodness Carol took charge."

It showed Carol with the Spirit Spoiler again. The next scene, bathed in red light, was the bogeyman melting away.

"Once again," Nick said, "the Ghost Stalkers were on the job."

Malcolm slumped. He was right. His heroes were nothing but actors putting on a fancy show.

"Those weasels!" Grandma Eunice shouted. She turned to Malcolm. "I can't believe they had the nerve to cut you out completely."

"Yeah," Dandy agreed. "Maybe you should write them another letter."

The next scene showed the Ghost Stalkers sitting on the couch. "Tune in next week," Carol said, "when we show off some new equipment."

The camera zoomed in on Nick. He held up a device that looked like a high-tech blow-dryer. "Like our new Ghost Stalkers Electromagnetic Ghost Finder."

Malcolm smiled. "I don't need to write any more letters. It looks like they finally got the message."

Questions for You

From Ghost Detectors
Malcolm and Dandy

Dandy: Malcolm and I were super excited for SciCon. Have you ever looked forward to something for a really long time? What was it?

Malcolm: Grandma Eunice is a spunky old lady. Do you have relatives who are as silly as she is? What funny things do they do?

Malcolm: I thought the stars of *Ghost Stalkers* were so cool . . . until I met them. Do you admire any TV or movie stars? Why do you look up to them? What do you think they would be like in real life?

Dandy: Malcolm and I worked together to zap the SciCon ghost. If you were in our shoes, would you have done it differently? What would you have done?